THIS CANDLEWICK BOOK BELONGS TO:

_____

_____

_____

_____

For Caroline and Sumner
M. W.

For my nephews,
Kevin, Patrick, and Alex
A. R.

Text copyright © 1996 by Martin Waddell
Illustrations copyright © 1996 by Arthur Robins

First U.S. paperback edition 1998

The Library of Congress has cataloged the
hardcover edition as follows:

Waddell, Martin.
What use is a moose? / by Martin Waddell ;
illustrated by Arthur Robins. — 1st U.S. ed.
p. cm.
Summary: When Jack's efforts to find a use for the moose
he has brought home end in disaster, Jack's mother says the moose
has to go — until she realizes that being loved is the best use of all.
ISBN 1-56402-933-6 (hardcover)
[1. Moose — Fiction.] I. Robins, Arthur, ill. II. Title.
PZ7.W1137Wg   1996
[E] — dc20   95-36138

ISBN 0-7636-0461-5 (paperback)

2 4 6 8 10 9 7 5 3 1

Printed in Hong Kong

This book was typeset in M Ellington.
The pictures were done in watercolor.

Candlewick Press
2067 Massachusetts Avenue
Cambridge, Massachusetts 02140

What Use Is a Moose?

by
Martin Waddell

illustrated by
Arthur Robins

CANDLEWICK PRESS
CAMBRIDGE, MASSACHUSETTS

Jack made friends with a moose in the woods, so he brought the moose back to his house.

"What use is a moose?" asked Jack's mom.

"I'm sure mooses have uses," said Jack.

"If you find a use for your moose, he can stay," said Jack's mom.

Jack and his moose sat in the yard
and thought.

"I could hang the wash on you to dry,
Moose," Jack suggested. So he hung
the wash on the moose. But . . .

That was no use!

"Can you drive, Moose? You could be Mom's chauffeur!" Jack said to the moose. But . . .

That was no use!

"Maybe you could work in the garden!"
said Jack. But . . .

That was no use!

"Could you make Mom
her dinner?" Jack asked
the moose. But . . .

Even that was no use!

"Your moose is wrecking our house!"
Mom told Jack, and she got very angry.
"We've no use for a moose!" she said.
"He'll have to go back to the woods."

Jack was upset. So was the moose. "You must be of some use," Jack told the moose.

So the moose did his best to help around the house.

"Oh, no!" said Mom.

"Not that way!" said Mom.

"No, no, no!" cried Mom.

"OH, *NOOOOOOO!*"

CRUNCH

"You're a very bad moose!" said Mom, pulling Jack up from the floor.

The moose shivered and quivered and shook.

"Get out of my house!" Mom told the moose. "You're no use and I don't want you here anymore!"

The moose went away.

Jack cried and cried for his moose.
"That moose was no use!" said his mom.
"But I *love* my moose," Jack told Mom.

Mom thought a little, then she said,
"You're right, Jack. Being loved is a
very good use for a moose." And she
called the moose back.

The moose stayed with Jack almost forever, but not in the house. It lived in a special moose shack out back, built by Jack . . .

and the moose!

MARTIN WADDELL is one of the most prolific and successful children's writers of his time, having written more than one hundred books for children, including *Can't You Sleep, Little Bear?*; *Let's Go Home, Little Bear*; *You and Me, Little Bear*; *Farmer Duck*; *Owl Babies*; and *When the Teddy Bears Came*. He has won numerous awards for his work, which *The Horn Book* has deemed "deliciously sly" and *School Library Journal* has called "outrageous and funny."

ARTHUR ROBINS has illustrated a number of children's books, including *Little Rabbit Foo Foo*, by Michael J. Rosen; *The Last Chocolate Cookie*, by Jamie Rix; *Knee-High Norman*, by Laurence Anholt; and the family series *Where Did I Come From?* and *What's Happening to Me?*, by Peter Mayle.